Why do I my teeth?

Contents

Written by Sally Morgan

Illustrated by Janos Jantner

Collins

What's in this book?

Listen and say

mouth

teeth

dentist

Download the audio at www.collins.co.uk/peapoddownloads

brush

electric toothbrush

toothpaste

4

Chapter 1 We need our teeth

We eat a lot of different food: rice, potatoes, bread, cakes, meat, fruit, and vegetables.

We need our teeth to eat this food.

We put food in our mouth. We need our teeth to **chew** the food into small **pieces**.

Do you like apples? You **bite** into an apple with your teeth.

We need our teeth for other things, too.
We smile when we are happy. When we smile,
we show our teeth.

Teeth help us to talk, to say words, and to sing.

Chapter 2 Let's look at your teeth

Stand in front of a mirror and open your mouth. Now look at your teeth. How many teeth do you have? How many teeth are at the top of your mouth? How many are at the bottom?

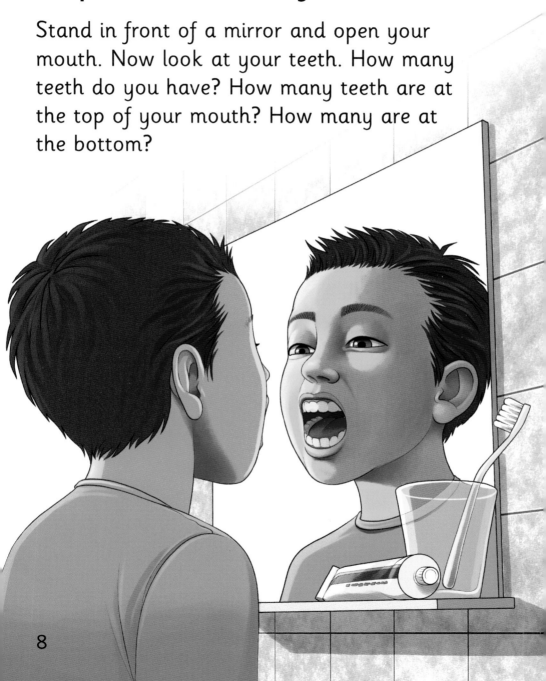

You have three different types of teeth. They are called incisors, canines, and molars. The incisors and canines are at the front of your mouth. These teeth bite your food.

Your molars are your largest teeth. They chew your food. Can you see them in your mouth?

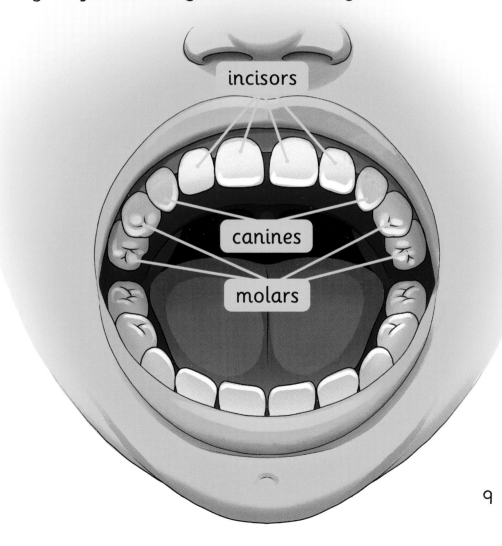

incisors

canines

molars

Chapter 3 Baby teeth

Very small babies don't have any teeth. They drink milk. They don't need teeth.

Babies grow their teeth when they're six months old. Their teeth help them to eat baby food.

A young child has 20 small teeth. These are called baby teeth.

Chapter 4 My tooth is wobbling!

It's exciting when your first tooth falls out. It usually **wobbles** first.

What do you do with your baby teeth when they fall out?

When baby teeth fall out, new teeth can grow. The new teeth **push** the baby teeth out.

These new teeth are called **adult teeth**.
They are bigger than the baby teeth.
When you are older, you have 32 adult teeth.

Chapter 5 Brushing your teeth

We often have pieces of food between our teeth after we eat. We brush our teeth to clean them. Clean teeth look good.

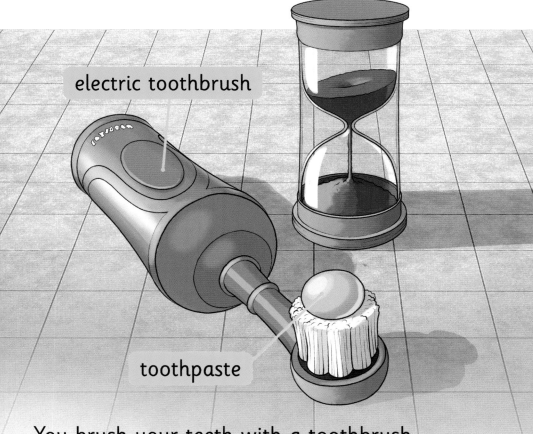

electric toothbrush

toothpaste

You brush your teeth with a toothbrush. What color is your toothbrush? Do you have an electric toothbrush?

Put a little toothpaste on your toothbrush. Then brush all your teeth. Move the toothbrush up and down for two minutes.

Brush your teeth in the morning and the evening. Don't eat or drink after you brush your teeth.

Chapter 6 Going to the dentist

A dentist **checks** that our teeth are OK.

We sit in a big chair and the dentist looks at all the teeth in our mouth.

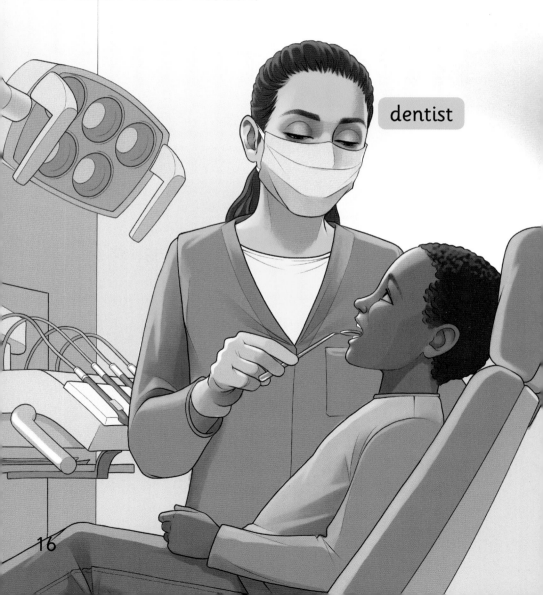

dentist

We enjoy eating sweet food, like cakes and chocolate. But these are not good for our teeth.

Germs like sweet things too, and germs grow on dirty teeth.

Teeth with a lot of germs on them can hurt. Sometimes they fall out. This isn't good.

Chapter 7 Do animals brush their teeth?

Animals need their teeth, too. Animals chew **hard** things to keep their teeth clean.

Dogs and big cats like chewing **bones**. These keep their teeth clean.

bone

Some people brush their pet's teeth. This person is brushing her cat's teeth.

Do you have a pet dog or cat? Do you brush their teeth?

Chapter 8 Some teeth don't stop growing

Our teeth grow when we are young, but then they stop growing.

Some animals have teeth that never stop growing. The teeth grow longer and longer. These are animals like hamsters, rats, mice, and rabbits.

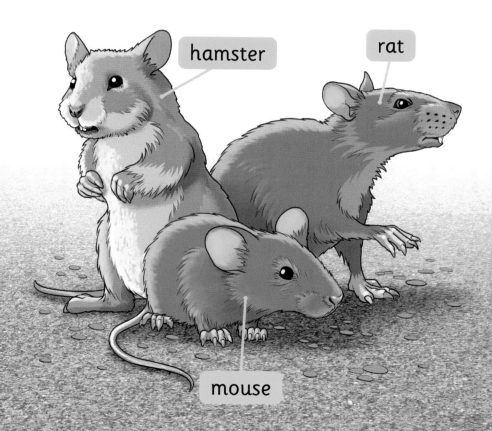

hamster

rat

mouse

These animals love to chew. This stops their teeth growing too long. Pet hamsters chew many things. Some people buy toys for their pets to chew.

rabbit

Chapter 9 A lot of teeth

Sharks are large fish that live in the sea.
They have many teeth in their mouths.
Can you see the teeth?

A shark has pointed teeth.

Sharks lose teeth every week. When one tooth falls out, a new tooth grows in its place.

Sharks can be 20 or 30 years old and grow many, many teeth.

a pointed tooth

Chapter 10 Big cats have big teeth!

Lions and tigers are big cats. Big cats eat meat.
They catch and hold their food with their teeth.
Lions have 30 teeth.

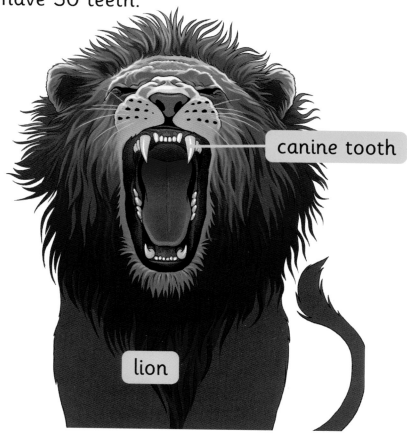

canine tooth

lion

Can you see the canine teeth?
These canines are really big!
How many canine teeth can you see?

This tiger is keeping its teeth clean. It chews on the bone. Its teeth are very strong.

tiger

Chapter 11 The biggest teeth

Some animals have huge teeth.

Elephants have two tusks. A tusk is a long incisor tooth. It grows to about two **meters** long. Elephant tusks are very strong. They use their tusks to find food.

tusk

Walruses have two tusks. These are canine teeth and grow to about a meter long. Walruses use their tusks to **pull** their bodies out of the water.

Narwhals live in cold water. They have one long tusk. This tooth is about three meters long. A narwhal's tusk helps it find fish to eat.

walrus

narwhal

Chapter 12 Be careful with your teeth

You need your teeth when you eat, too.

Sharks can grow new teeth, but you can't.
Always be careful with your teeth.

Don't eat too much candy. Brush your teeth in the mornings and at night. Go to the dentist once a year, or more.

Now smile and show me your beautiful teeth!

Mini-dictionary

Listen and read

adult teeth (plural noun)
Your **adult teeth** are
the teeth that grow in
your mouth after your
first baby teeth fall out.

bite (verb) When you **bite**
something, you use
your teeth to cut into it.

bone (noun) A **bone** is one
of the hard white parts
inside a person's or an
animal's body.

brush (verb) If you **brush**
your teeth, you
clean them with a
special brush.

check (verb) If someone
checks something, they
make sure that it is good.

chew (verb) When you
chew, you break food
with your teeth.

germ (noun) A **germ** is
a very small living
thing that can make
people sick.

hard (adjective) something
that is **hard**, is not easy
to bend, break, or cut.

meter (noun) You use
meters to talk about
how long something
is. There are 100
centimeters in a **meter**.

piece (noun) A **piece**
is one part of
something bigger.

pull (verb) If someone
or something **pulls**
another thing, they hold
it and use force to move
it closer.

push (verb) If someone
or something **pushes**
another thing, they
use force to make it
move away.

wobble (verb) When your
tooth **wobbles**, it
makes small movements
from left to right.

1 Look and match

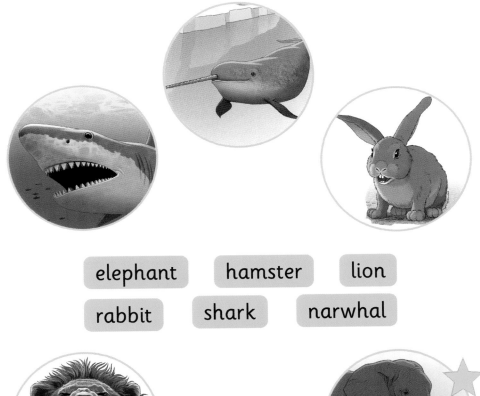

elephant   hamster   lion

rabbit   shark   narwhal

2 Listen and say

Collins

Published by Collins
An imprint of HarperCollins*Publishers*
Westerhill Road
Bishopbriggs
Glasgow
G64 2QT

HarperCollins*Publishers*
1st Floor, Watermarque Building
Ringsend Road
Dublin 4
Ireland

William Collins' dream of knowledge for all began with the publication of his first book in 1819.

A self-educated mill worker, he not only enriched millions of lives, but also founded a flourishing publishing house. Today, staying true to this spirit, Collins books are packed with inspiration, innovation, and practical expertise. They place you at the center of a world of possibility and give you exactly what you need to explore it.

© HarperCollins*Publishers* Limited 2021

10 9 8 7 6 5 4 3 2 1

ISBN 978-0-00-849035-5

Collins® and COBUILD® are registered trademarks of HarperCollins*Publishers* Limited

www.collins.co.uk/elt

British Library Cataloguing in Publication Data

A catalogue record for this publication is available from the British Library.

Author: Sally Morgan
Illustrator: Janos Jantner (Beehive)
Series editor: Rebecca Adlard
Commissioning editor: Zoë Clarke
Publishing manager: Lisa Todd
Product managers: Jennifer Hall and Caroline Green
In-house editor: Alma Puts Keren
Project manager: Emily Hooton
Editors: Matthew Hancock and Samantha Lacey
Proofreaders: Natalie Murray and Michael Lamb
Cover designer: Kevin Robbins
Typesetter: 2Hoots Publishing Services Ltd
Audio produced by White House Sound Ltd
Reading guide author: Emma Wilkinson
Production controller: Rachel Weaver
Printed and bound by: Pureprint Group, UK

Download the audio for this book and a reading guide for parents and teachers at www.collins.co.uk/peapoddownloads